With love to my favorite truckers, Emmett and Jack — J.P.

For my soulmates: Arsa and Bebus — T.B.

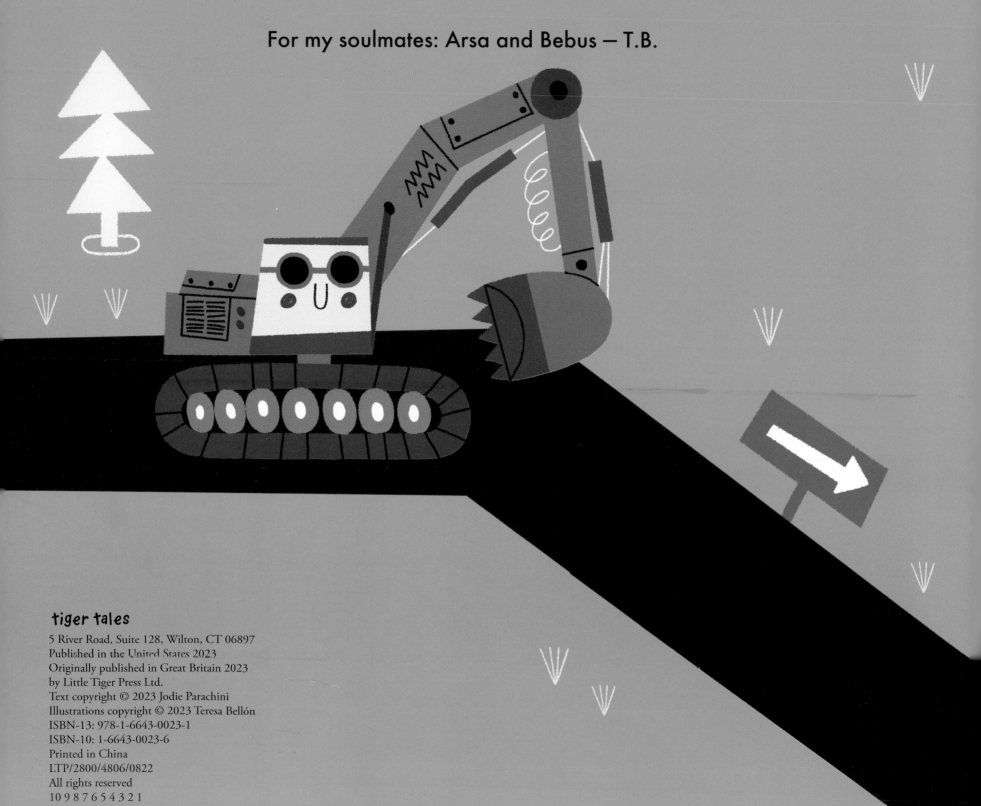

tiger tales

5 River Road, Suite 128, Wilton, CT 06897
Published in the United States 2023
Originally published in Great Britain 2023
by Little Tiger Press Ltd.
Text copyright © 2023 Jodie Parachini
Illustrations copyright © 2023 Teresa Bellón
ISBN-13: 978-1-6643-0023-1
ISBN-10: 1-6643-0023-6
Printed in China
LTP/2800/4806/0822
All rights reserved
10 9 8 7 6 5 4 3 2 1

www.tigertalesbooks.com

WAKE UP, TRUCKS!

by
Jodie Parachini

Illustrated by
Teresa Bellón

tiger tales

Wake up, trucks!

The day has begun.

It's time to have some trucking fun!

Open up your sleepy eyes.
No more resting. Time to rise!

Diggers like to eat and eat
when breakfast is a tasty treat.

Eggs and toast and bacon?

YUCK!

THAT'S not food to feed a truck!

Slurp some oil–power BLAST!
Now we're set for driving
FAST!

Follow School Bus down the street.

HONK!
at all the friends we meet.

One more left,
and then a right

to make it to the . . .

LET'S BEGIN!
We can't wait to dig right in.

Trucks don't learn their

A B C s

or how to count the

1 2 3s.

Desks and pencils? Crayons? **No!**

On this site
we tug
and tow.

Building cities—
that's our goal!

All the trucks have their own role.

Dump Truck carries heavy loads.

Roller is here to smooth the roads.

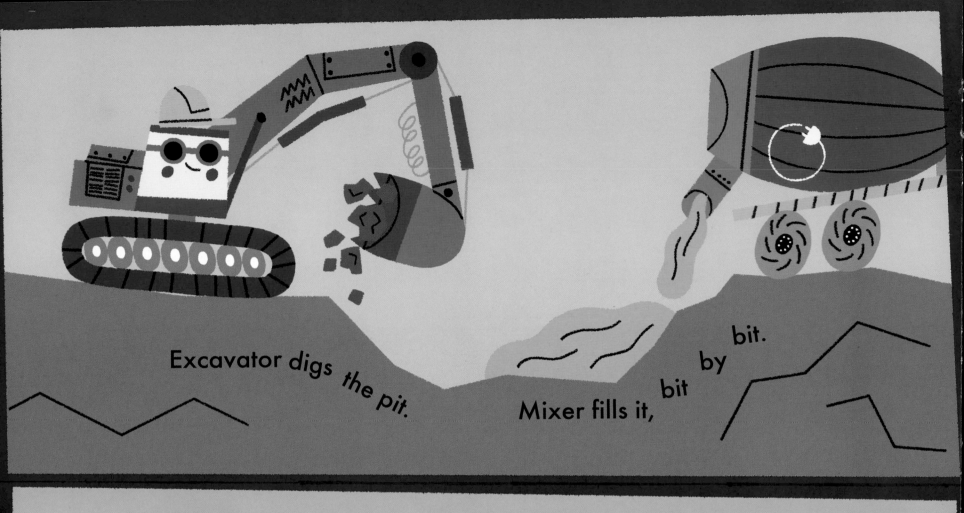

Excavator digs the pit.

Mixer fills it, bit by bit.

Here's the wood to line the floors.

Be careful, Loader, with the doors!

Bricks are in place and windows, too.
There's one last thing for the trucks to do . . . .

Mighty Crane, please hold it steady.
A roof at last!

The building is ready!

Hard hats off! Our job is done.
What do young trucks do for fun?

We don't need a slide or swings,
or a ball—none of those things!

Trucks just need a trusty crew.

We **love** friendship,
just like YOU!

The trucks line up; their day is done.
They head home in the setting sun.

Here's our exit. Good-bye, town.
Press the brakes.

We all slooooow down.

Spray us clean. Such dirty trucks!
Don't forget the rubber ducks.

Brush our grills and buff our lights.

Cool our engines. Say good nights.

Backing up? Please stop your beeping!
All your friends are busy sleeping.
Parked and peaceful, eyes are closing.

Mixer slumbers. Dozer's dozing.
Resting, snoozing, calm, and still,

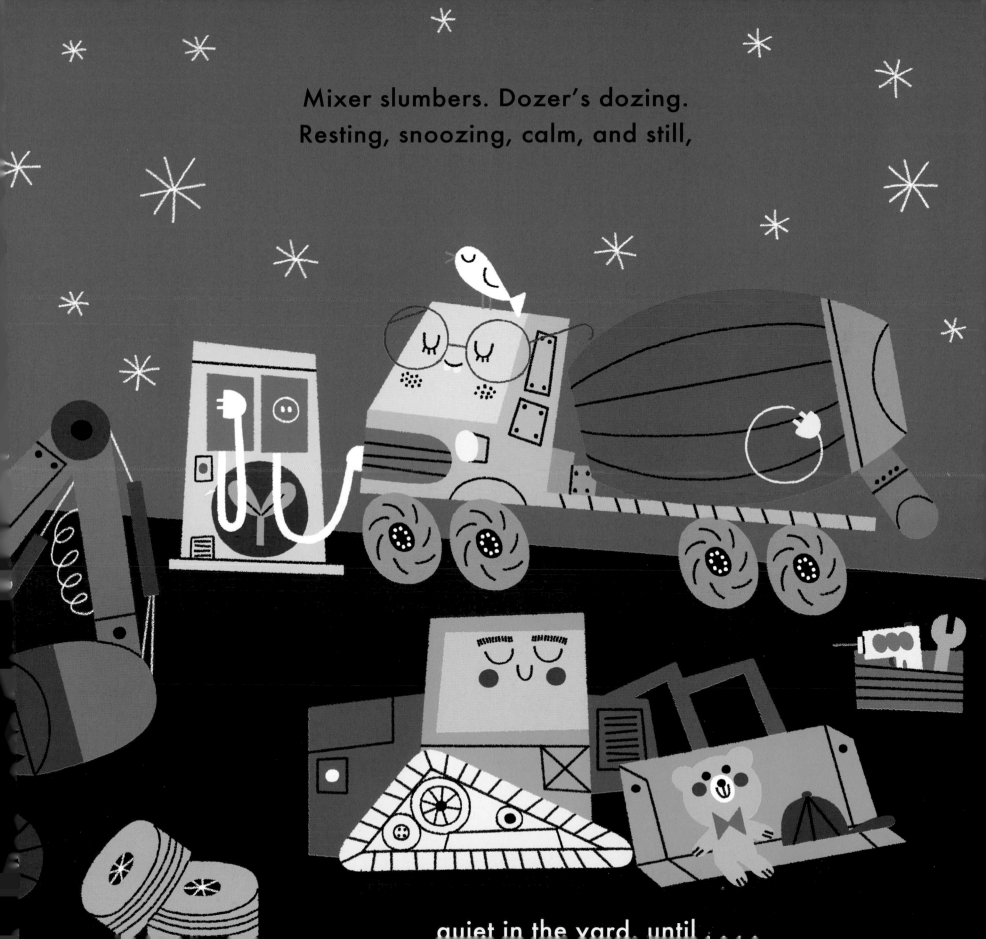

quiet in the yard, until

Wake up, trucks!

A new day dawns.

Shift your gears and stifle yawns.
Haul up! Hoist up! Rise and shine.
Grab your friends—it's trucking time!